YOU KNOW NOTHING

RUI LIMA

2019

©

I know nothing too.

You know as much as I do if you know nothing.

Nothing, you know.

Knowing nothing is better of what I must know.

I must know nothing to know as much we do.

We can and we most.

The future belongs to its intentions, not to us.

When my brain upgrades information, it deducts aberration and multiples common sense.

I exist formidably.

Remember we are not alone.
Even stars have planets.

**Nothing can stop opportunity from happening
or cause to solidify.**

The importance of any subject is equal to its needs.

I am poor of life when dying of old age.

Temporarily we dismiss life and embrace death into final transformation.

When you squeeze and measure your sentiment under pressure, you exist greatly.

Nothing is everlasting like the past that never departed.

Forever young may you stay smiling at your older soul.

Wisdom may you breathe, tender cause of all.

The incredible way to waste time is to talk about time wasted.

Live life softly. You will not regret.

**The path to eternity starts with the first sin
and the last breath.**

A mistake may imitate disabled righteous intention.

We have been loved at least once.

True love exists in reality and into a fantasy world.

Crying may be the solution to pain or the result of it. Cry if you have to, as much you need to feel satisfied.

Do not mediate with fouls when they are breathing.

Fragile is what breaks without intention.

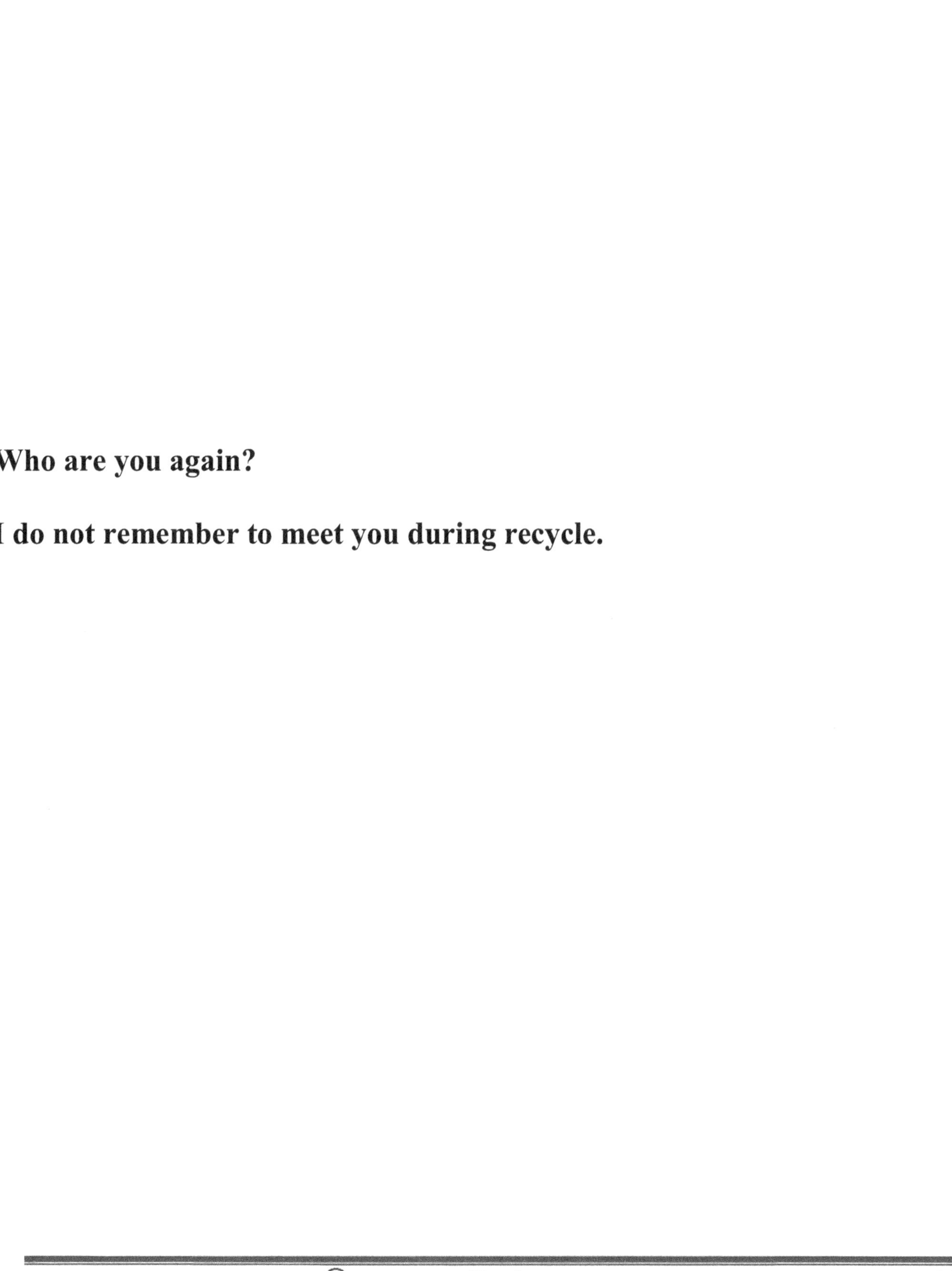

Who are you again?

I do not remember to meet you during recycle.

The average experiences are cursed.

I am blue and red.

Purple sometimes.

Reality is the concept describing what is perceived by the norm.

There is no reality like yours.

Do not disturb the peaceful mind of an angry animal.

The consequences may result in expiration.

A fantastic trip ends when a boring life starts.

We are unbearable to our own mistakes.

Treat them with solutions.

Not all winners won.

Not all losers lost.

The future belongs to its determination
and hidden knowledge.

What demons do you have?

Knowing encourages the ability to disciple them.

The gate to flames and eternal pain is larger than the path to heaven.

**Take me to my master and he will enlighten
who I am.**

What do you know of love and hate?

What do you know of life and death?

What do you know about you?

The spring and the winter are the same under the sun.

You are the only one too.

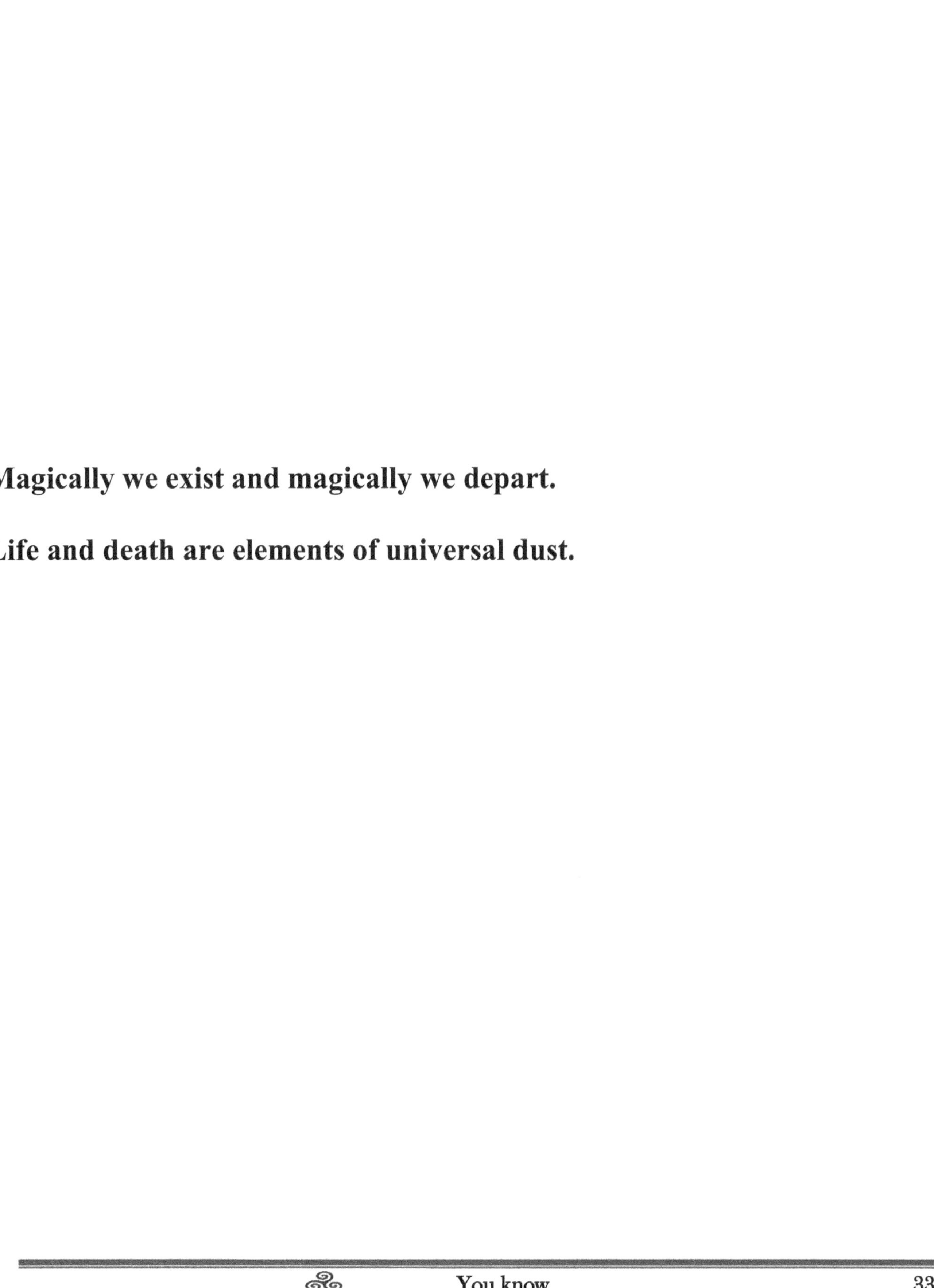

Magically we exist and magically we depart.

Life and death are elements of universal dust.

Far away is where I stand from myself
sometimes.

We can generate distance from the truth as long we are capable of
ignoring possibilities.

The universe belongs to travelers.

Progress intimidates and imagination insults limited people.

I know that in order to depart eternally from this planet, I must be genuinely and consistently good,
and unselfishly express love and care.

I remember your eyes into my eyes.
I remember your soul from the past.

You do not recognize me.

Maybe we will meet again.

Seek liberation from the belief system tattooed on your brain.

Your mind is the destination of every certain and uncertain thought you had or may have.

Stay free.
Remain within freedom.

How many times did we love the unknown?

I miss loving unfairly measuring pain and pleasure.

I mentioned you in my dreams.
Reality is surrealistically abnormal.

Once again
I sleep intentionally seeking happiness.

A touch…
My arm remained paralyzed.

Shy once again I stayed.

Age permits and takes away.

I am not the enemy.
You need to know that.

I care about all the matters searching happiness.

Let me tell you a story about love and pain.
Let me laugh, cry and entertain.

No one is far from their own destiny.

Some of us are only travelling far from our own true destination.

I like your eyes when in mine.
Light travels into my darkness.

You are dangerous to my insanity.

I cannot pretend to love you.

I am awful pretending when I love.

Time takes and gives.
Time masters and kills.

Time becomes and time is no more.
Time is an illusion of all.

Time does not exist.
Time measures life.

Time is what we have.
Time is what we don't have.

What is time?

Time is the most precious element of all.

A moment of sadness and silence takes
self-understanding away.

A funeral room empty of happiness.
A crying singing of tears.

I laid down in flowers and ants, watching from above
departing from an old body.

Addiction creates suffering.

I understand.
I acknowledge.
I admit.
I accept.

Addiction creates suffering.
The search for pleasure ends in sorrow.

Loss.
Confusion.
Shame.
Guilt.
Death.

Recycle.

Denial is what is and what appears not to be.
Minimizations.
Justifications.
Rationalizations.
Futile aberrations covering doors of insanity.
Greed.
Hatred.
Delusion.
Unworthy feelings avoided.
Anguish.
Misery.
Imbalance.
Pain.
We know nothing but suffering.
Anger.
Resentment.
Jealousy.
Envy.

Accept.
Change.
Cure.
Live free.

Die.

Caring takes a lot of work and patient.

I cannot care more than what patient permits.

I crave laughing.
What a great way to go through life.

Laughing is a permanent necessity.

What is life without genuine laughing?

The moment we laughed together
I knew I would have feelings for you.

The moment you made me smile
I knew I would be able to love you.

Your Old soul is just like mine.
Travelling in the mundane region of the universe.
Seeking to upgrade immensely.

False and fake people act the same way.

Recognize them by their peculiar eyes
and corrupted teeth.

Stereotyping is a regular phenomenon.
A gift from the Gods to foul humans.

My tall shadow moved in front of me.
Rushed into the cold April morning,
Reminding me of superb light…

I measured the aptitude of my thoughts
And sat quietly under the fig tree.

I looked and felt the awaking sun…
and received perpetual enlightenment.

- I am ready to consume the sun and the rain
- I am ready to return home.

Demons attempt to corrupt our ways of life.

Use them to work for your own benefit.

Do not become disciplined by them.

Discipline your demons.

You are their master.

Believe.

Apply.

Know.

As a zoo keeper I used to maintain the coordination
between unstable flamingos, self-important pink panthers, and other
usable species.

Sleep apnea will be my killer if I don't wake up.

There are two types of medical doctors
the good and the bad.

Always seek the best for your needs.

I am from the moon.

Where are you from?

We remain delusional for the children.

We can and we must.

Temporarily we exist.
Temporarily we continue ourselves.

Nothing is permanent.

Not even you.

Intentionally we have the key of the universe and the ability to its door.

We know more when we define.

Adjusting facilitates purposes and beautifies beginnings.

I was born to die someday.
Hopefully not today.

God has more irony than the greatest storm.

I met people and their pets.
Great species to remember unconditionally.

We simply knew nothing about ourselves until
we discovered how to feel correctly.

**Arrogant people take the best of my behaviors
and the worst of my tolerance.**

I cannot support stupidity as much I support compassion.

Initiate the best of you anytime provocation occurs.
It is worthy to consistently breathe when swimming.

What is balance without seeking the true?
What is love without perpetual karma?
What is hate without periodical death?

How much are we from what we become?

Nothing is less important of what didn't happen.
Everything manifests the importance of its shape.

We pretend to care about so much and nothing.
We fake a smile and a conversation.
We seek pleasure and pain.

We are humans and animals.
We are not forever.

Existence equals calculated mortality.

Freedom arrives with the last breathe.

We are similar to dust, nothing.

The knowledge of a wise person curiously starves
for the complexity and understanding of everything, and from nothing
completely certain.

We don't care as much you think.
The drama of caring does not have
limitations for love.

Love is the test and the test is love.
Nothing builds, rebuilds or destroys like love.

I miss your tears running down my face and your lips close to mine. I simply miss you.

Misery is great served cold in a raining day.

The train took me to unknown places where plastic flowers and robotic people pretended to care.

**My plan is to get there by conquering any challenge
and challenging any hurdle.**

Nothing is more important that breathing and caring.

We are not the only ones looking at the universe for answers and questions. We are certainly the only ones with more questions than answers.

Nothing is genuinely uncertain until it manifests turmoil.

Agree or disagree are foundations of imbecility.

I loved and love.
I cared and care.

These states of mind transformed my life to uncontrollably laughing and sublime understanding.

I exist for a purpose.

I am now.

Reality is a dimension into others dimensions.

We travel uninterruptedly between imagination
and reality.

We travel sleeping and awaking.
We are real and we are not always here.

We are only able to pretend to be conscious if we are unable to define ourselves.

Knowing is power as believing is virtue.

Politicians can also be snakes, lambs and crocodiles.

We may measure virtue with kindness and sorry with pity.

Luck has no interest in everybody willing to get it.

Do not get away from what you are. Your destination is into you. Find it and care for as long as you breathe.

Love what you feel to love. Do not stop loving what you must. Nothing or no one is capable of stopping you for loving.

We are the unknown and its location.

Virtually the world shows more liars than stars.

My intentions were purely to understand your determination to remain constantly miserable.

Why do you abuse yourself daily?

Self-compassion is what you need.

By understanding your life experiences, and by finding your strengths
and hope, may or may not result in your true intentions to gain self-love.

Do not assault the healthy thoughts of a good friend with devilish sarcasm and punitive words. Remember that Karma is intentionally a protector of good in this world.

A genuine foul brings foulness and judgment.

I met educated people with no common sense or functional brain.

I had enough realization of everything and everyone carefully conditioned, when I recognized how absurd and delusional society became.

Before I depart from this boldly world,
I will learn, believe and know how to find you.

Careless thoughts remain considerable accessible to impulsive people.

Success is designed by birth and killed by choice.

Even the disorganized wind has a purpose.

Do you know the differences between knowing and not understanding? Can you provide an example?

Love unconditionally every day and one more day.

We are made of puzzles and ashes.

Nothing is completely abnormal to understand in a materialistic world.

I like the sun entering my veins and rain covering my body. I am the humanly seed rebirthing within the impure soil.

We sat near of the ocean waves holding our bodies on the dark sand. The island had water and food until our eternity. We were uniquely amazed by love.

I can travel to your insanity more than once a week, but never forever. I coexist appropriately when insane.

The physics of the universe are continually unknown. Knowing more equals knowing less. Nothing is known artificially or completely.

Laughing is above contentment.

A small conversation connects wasteful time with common symbolism.

The one who cares about nothing is genuinely free.

**When we start limiting ourselves,
we become conditionally limited.**

Become what you must. Acquire courage.

Chaos is not free.

Remember,
 sometimes uncommon noises get the attention of the universe.

Let be and know to be. Everything else will take the exact planned symmetry.